Colin Payne is a postman from Bristol, where he has lived for most of his life. He has two children of a bothersome age and a partner whose age shall not be mentioned.

i

The Hiccuppy Puppy

COLIN PAYNE

AUSTIN MACAULEY PUBLISHERS™

LONDON • CAMBRIDGE • NEW YORK • SHARJAH

ISBN 9781035834259 (Paperback)
ISBN 9781035834266 (Hardback)
ISBN 9781035834273 (ePub e-book)

www.austinmacauley.com

First Published 2024
Austin Macauley Publishers Ltd®
1 Canada Square
Canary Wharf
London
E14 5AA

To Lois, Poppy and Rosie,
Thank you.

And Tiggy Dog.

Mum, Dad, Christine, Dave and Kevin. All the Morrells – Rudy, Lou, Joan, Kevin, Ciaran and Ben. All my friends – Ryan, Steve, Carey, Rich and Moo. My work colleagues. Everybody on my postal duty around Totterdown who read this silly story and encouraged me to get it published.

Yawn and stretch the puppy did do when he awoke
from his slumber,
What to do today, the doggie did wonder.
First, I'll eat the food in my bowl
Followed by digging a nice big hole!!!

And then I think a little nap
Preferably on someone's lap.
So up he got, but soon did stop, rather abrupt
For from his gut, a strange noise did erupt!
It was an enormous rumble
And a huge grumble
That arose from his belly
It made him wobble like a great big jelly
It shook him to his very core
The likes of which the pup had never felt before
Up it came faster and faster
Try to stop it he just couldn't master,
So out it came, a noise like no other
Quickly followed by another and another.

HICCUP! HICCUP! HICCUP!

The puppy did freeze,
What was he to do? Would somebody help him, please?
He looked around
But no one was found
And still, those hiccups wouldn't back down!!

HICCUP! HICCUP! HICCUP!

He hiccupped on the bed!!!
He hiccupped on his head!!!
He hiccupped on the floor!!!
He even hiccupped out of the door!!!
And when he finally thought that was that
He hiccupped next to the neighbour's cat!!!

The cat jumped in such a shock
It landed on top of the grandfather clock!!!
"Oh," said the cat. "You silly, silly pup
Can't you get those hiccups to stop?"

"No, I can't," hiccupped the dog
Who bizarrely had hiccupped on top of a great big frog!!!
And that's no joke
The frog did croak.
The cat climbed down
With a great big frown
And said to the pup
"If you want them to stop
Drink from a cup
Upside down, you must sup."

HICCUP! HICCUP! HICCUP!

The dog did wonder
To drink from under?
That was a lot to ask
Could he do such a task?
A cup he had found
Great big red and round
So the best form of attack
Was to lie on his back
He crawled up to the mug
Upside down like a slug
And feeling quite smug
He took a big glug

HICCUP! HICCUP! HICCUP!

The cup tipped up
All over the pup
All over his head, all over his fur
What happened next was a bit of a blur
He ran out of the house
Tripped over a mouse
Rolled down the hill
And in a pile of mud, he finally came still!
All was quiet; nothing was heard
Had those blasted hiccups disappeared?

HICCUP! HICCUP! HICCUP!

Out from the mud, the puppy did crawl
So upset he started to bawl
"That cat was no help at all
I think he played a joke on me, made me look small
To stop these hiccups, I must on my own
I'll start by looking in that traffic cone."
He poked his head in bit by bit
Oh my, what a tight fit!!
Of all the rotten luck
His silly head had only gotten stuck
He shook it to the left; he shook it to the right
He shook it so hard he almost took flight!!
But try as he might
That cone was stuck tight!
Probably for the rest of the night

HICCUP! HICCUP! HICCUP!

Oh, finally, some luck
The cone had come unstuck
He had hiccupped himself free
And landed up a tree
Down he climbed in one big mess
How he liked these hiccups less and less
All covered in mud, twigs, leaves and brambles
He headed back home in a bit of a shambles

No more for me; enough is enough
If these hiccups don't go, well, that's just tough!
As he walked up to his bed
He had a feeling of dread!!
For he caught a glimpse of something in the mirror
The pup edged towards it, ever nearer and nearer
Not sure what he'd see
Not sure what it would be
Oh my, what a sight!
It gave the puppy a massive fright

He ran away and dived under his cover
Shaking all over, wondering if he'd ever recover
The pup poked his head out
But no one was about
He looked around
Nobody, nothing, not even a sound
Not even a hiccup
Not even a **HICCUP!**
Not even a **HICCUP!**
Oh finally! At long last, the hiccups had gone, and he
was a very, very happy puppy.

AITCHOO!